For T.W. D.S.

To Lin, with love G.B.

A NOTE ABOUT THE ART

Gary Blythe did most of his research on the Native Americans depicted in this book at the South Dakota State Historical Society in Pierre. In addition, The National Museum of the American Indian at the Smithsonian Institution supplied copies of original photographs of clothing, horses, ponies, and artifacts. Mr. Blythe also used several books for reference, the key one being *The Sioux of the Rosebud: A History in Pictures* by Jean T. Hamilton and Henry W. Hamilton, photographs by John A. Anderson (University of Oklahoma Press, 1980). The countryside in the art is based on sketches drawn and photographs taken by Mr. Blythe in South Dakota. The paintings are oil on canvas.

First published in the United States 1994
by Dial Books for Young Readers
A Division of Penguin Books USA Inc.
375 Hudson Street
New York, New York 10014
Published in Great Britain 1993 by Hutchinson Children's
Books as *The Garden*
Text copyright © 1993 by Dyan Sheldon
Paintings copyright © 1993 by Gary Blythe
All rights reserved
Typography by Julie Rauer
Printed in Singapore by Tien Wah Press (Pte) Ltd
1 3 5 7 9 10 8 6 4 2

Library of Congress Cataloging in Publication Data
Sheldon, Dyan.
Under the moon / by Dyan Sheldon ; paintings by Gary Blythe.
p.   cm.
Summary: After finding an arrowhead in her backyard,
a young girl has a dream about what the area was once like.
ISBN 0-8037-1670-2
[1. Indians of North America—Fiction. 2. Dreams—Fiction.]
I. Blythe, Gary, ill. II. Title.
PZ7.S54144Un 1994 [E]—dc20 93-11711 CIP AC

UNDER THE MOON

BY DYAN SHELDON
PAINTINGS BY GARY BLYTHE

DIAL BOOKS FOR YOUNG READERS
NEW YORK

Jenny found a stone while she was digging in her backyard. It was dark and rough and came to a point. She had never seen anything like it before.

"Look at this," said Jenny. "I think it must be a magic stone."

Jenny's mother smiled. "That's not a magic stone. It's a flint." She touched it with her finger. "It might even be an arrowhead. It could be hundreds of years old."

Jenny looked all around her. There were beds of flowers against the fence, and a fish pond in one corner. Beyond her yard there were houses and streetlights and busy roads; and beyond them the stores of the town, and then the buildings of the city.

"What was it like here hundreds of years ago?" asked Jenny.

Her mother took the stone and turned it over in her hand. "There were no roads, no cars, no cities, and no towns. Just the people, the animals, and the land itself," she said.

It was hard for Jenny to imagine what it must have been like when there were forests instead of cities, and fields instead of towns.

But then, far in the distance Jenny thought she saw a man on horseback, looking as though he might ride into the clouds. She blinked, and the man disappeared.

Jenny's mother handed her the piece of flint and they talked of how the world had been when the land was as large and as open as the sky, of hunting on the plains and in the mountains and forests, of singing, and telling stories by firelight.

Jenny stayed outside all afternoon. She tried to picture people riding their horses across the faraway hills. But all she saw were the cars and trucks racing along the busy road.

She tried to picture young men hunting in the high grass of the plains, their movements slow and their weapons ready. But all she saw was the cat stalking through the flowers and her mother's shrubs.

As dusk blurred the shapes in the garden and the yard, Jenny thought she could hear the voices of women bent over their fires; the voices were soft and laughing. But it was only the radio in the house next door.

Jenny was still outside when the moon came up.

"Jenny," called her mother from the house, "come on in. It's getting dark."

But Jenny pretended not to hear. She wanted to stay where she was, watching and imagining.

Later she asked if she could sleep in her tent, the way people used to sleep in their tepees.

Jenny's mother sighed. "All right," she said. "But we must put your tent close to the house so I can keep an eye on you."

Jenny lay awake for a long time that night. She listened for the howling of wolves and gazed out at the stars. She stared at the sky so hard that she thought she saw a trail of clouds turn into buffalo and race across the moon. When she finally did fall asleep, the arrowhead was still fast in her hand.

Jenny had a dream.

She dreamed that she woke in the night. From somewhere close by came the murmur of low voices.

When she cautiously opened the flap of her tent, the world outside had changed.

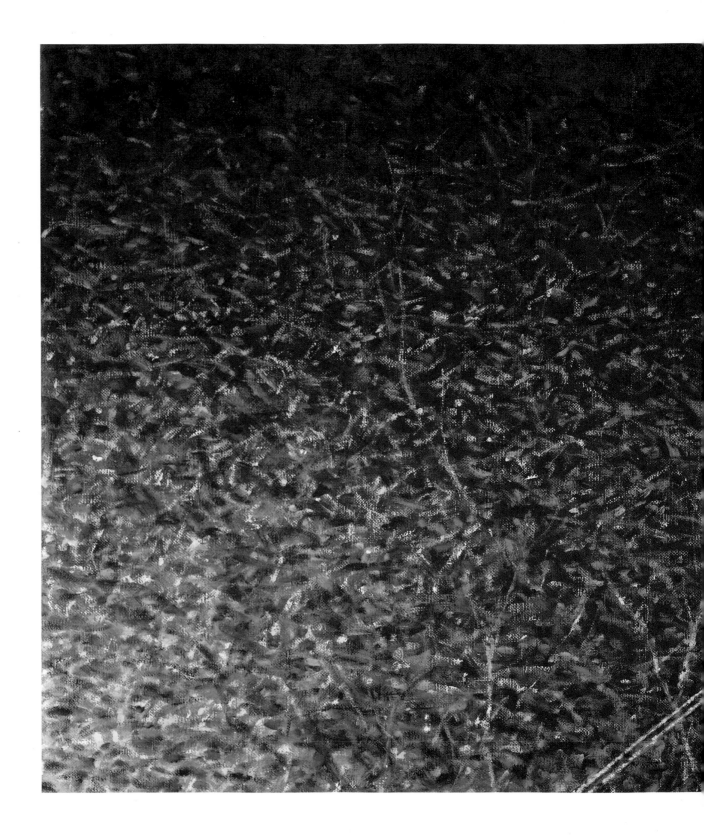

The moon was corn-yellow and the stars sat low in a blue-black sky.

There were no houses or lights, no roads and no cars. In the distance rose rolling hills. Where the town had stood there were fields of grass. Night birds called and the trees rustled. Jenny's house and yard were gone.

She looked around in wonder. There were ponies where the vegetable patch should have been, and dogs dozing where the flowers had grown. In place of the fish pond was a whispering stream. Painted tepees stood in a clearing, smoke drifting past them like clouds. And there, not far from her, a circle of people sat around a fire, their voices soft.

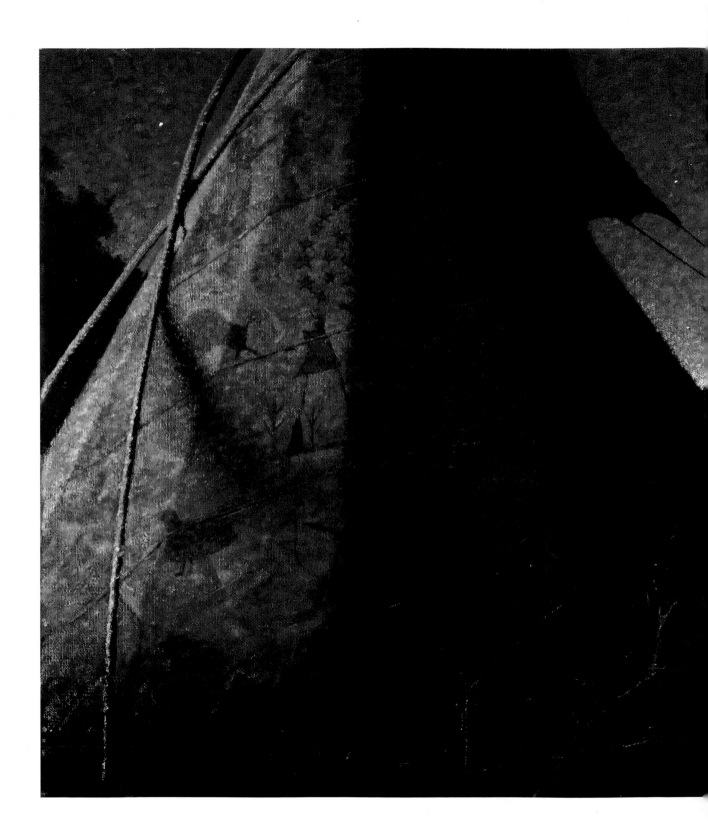

One of the men turned and looked toward Jenny. He beckoned to her.

Because it was a dream, Jenny knew what he wanted. He wanted her to return his arrowhead.

The dogs began to bark as Jenny crawled from her tent, but because she was dreaming, she wasn't afraid. She crossed to the fire.

The man moved over and Jenny sat down. She placed the arrowhead in his hand.

Jenny sat in the circle all through the night, while the drum played, and the flute sounded, and they told her how the world had been, so long ago, when the land was as large and as open as the sky. When there were stories in the stars and songs in the sun. When every thing on earth had a voice and a heart, and time was measured by the changings of the moon.

In the morning, when Jenny really woke up, the flowers were still growing along the fence. The cars were still speeding past on the busy road. The arrowhead was still in her hand.

Jenny stared beyond her backyard. Clouds drifted past the sun like smoke. The beating of her heart recalled the drumming of her dream.

Without a sound Jenny crept from her tent. At the edge of the yard she knelt in the grass, and buried the arrowhead back in the earth. And just for an instant, in the shimmering light, Jenny saw the world as it once was...so long ago, when the land was as large and as open as the sky.